CERTIFICATE OF BIRTH

DT 884726

For Mimi, Zen, Stan and Ember — B. F.

For Emma and Goldy — D. T.

Bloomsbury Publishing, London, Oxford, New York, New Delhi and Sydney
First published in Great Britain in 2017 by Bloomsbury Publishing Plc
50 Bedford Square, London WC1B 3DP

www.bloomsbury.com

BLOOMSBURY is a registered trademark of Bloomsbury Publishing Plc

Text copyright © Ben Faulks 2017
Illustrations copyright © David Tazzyman 2017

The moral rights of the author and illustrator have been asserted

A CIP catalogue record for this book is available from the British Library

ISBN 978 1 4088 6724 2 (HB)
ISBN 978 1 4088 6725 9 (PB)
ISBN 978 1 4088 8332 7 (eBook)

All papers used by Bloomsbury Publishing are natural, recyclable products made from wood grown in
well managed forests. The manufacturing processes conform to the environmental regulations of the country of origin

Printed in China by Leo Paper Products, Heshan, Guangdong

1 3 5 7 9 10 8 6 4 2

What MAKES me a ME?

BEN FAULKS

illustrated by
DAVID TAZZYMAN

BLOOMSBURY
LONDON OXFORD NEW YORK NEW DELHI SYDNEY

"Who am I?"
I ask myself.
"What makes me
a **ME**?"

I think hard with all my might
and look around to see.

At times I can be like a snail.

I go so very SLOW.

It makes my mum go beserk.

"We're LATE," she says.

"Let's GO!"

But...

MY eyes don't stand out on stalks
and snails are far TOO slimy.
And though we've both got backpacks,
it's clear that mine's more SHINY.

Hey, LOOK, I'm like
my jumper –
we're exactly the
same size.

Same shaped tummy,
same shaped arms.
AND we're both
aged five!

But...

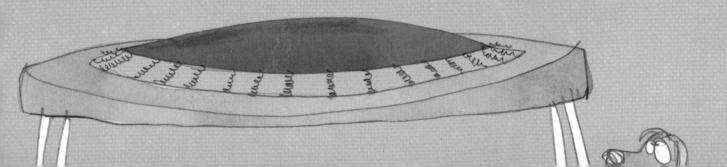

My jumper is a **lazybones**.
It's sad to say
but TRUE.

You see, it won't do **anything**
unless I do it TOO.

My dad says I'm like Alfie Wilks,
the boy who lives next door.
Together we play DINOSAURS
that
STOMP
and
CHOMP
and

ROAR!

But...

Mum will often tell me,
and she'll look me in the eye.
"You're NOT to be like Alfie Wilks."
I really don't know why.

Perhaps I'm like my puppy dog.
We're always FULL of beans.
When Monty drops his bouncy ball,
I know just what he means.

But, wait a minute...

WHERE'S my tail?
Of course, I haven't got one.
And Monty loves to chew on bones,
but I don't call that fun!

Am I like a **tree**? Maybe!

My arms stick out like branches.

And when the wind

BLOWS us about

we both do

funny dances.

But...

Trees are rooted to the spot,

while I run here and there.

Though sometimes

my Dad tells me...

I've got
birds' nests
in my hair!

Sometimes I'm like a sports car.

Neeeeee-awwww!

I'm *LIGHTNING* fast.

I'm cool round corners,

BRAVE round bends,

I DON'T like coming last.

But ...

I use my legs to *ZOOM* along,

NOT wheels that spin about.

And cars can only HONK and beep,

while I can scream and SHOUT.

Of course, I'm LOTS like Super Guy.
We're BOTH so strong and BRAVE.

We help the goodies
fight the baddies,

and have the
world to SAVE.

But...

Super Guy, I'm not sure why,
LOVES to kiss the girls.

HE has *SLEEK* and shiny hair,
while I have knots
and CURLS.

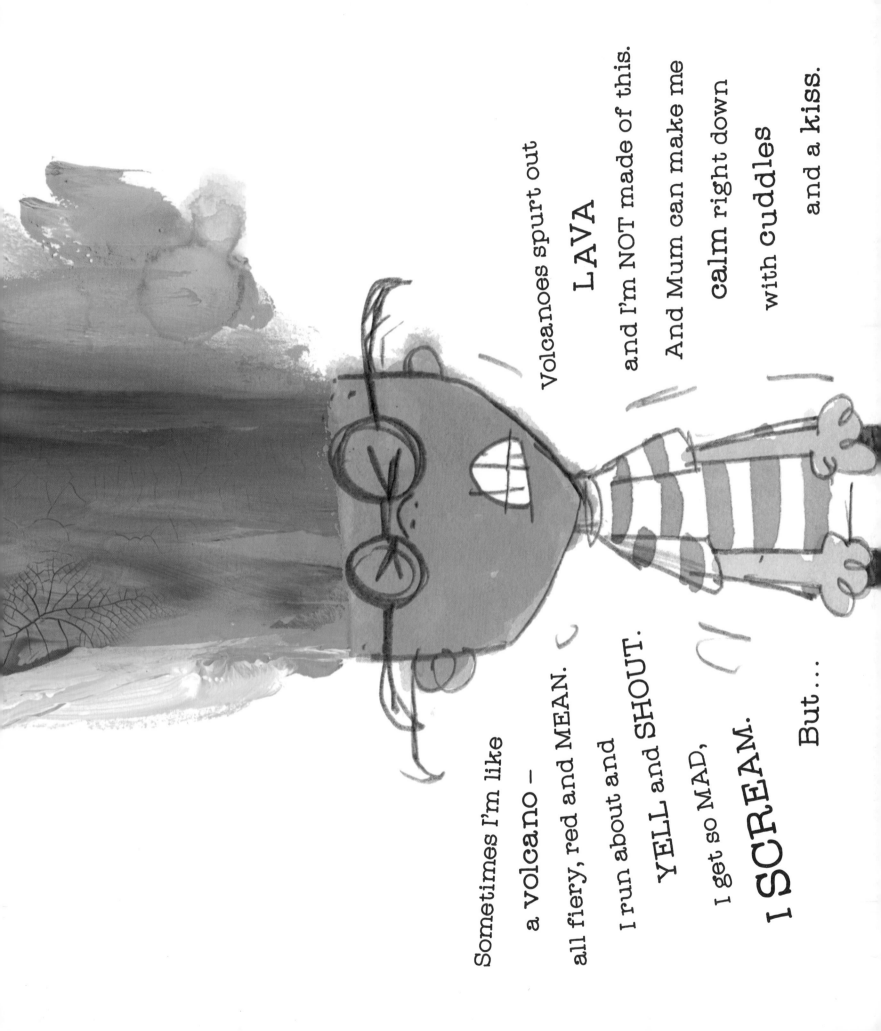

Sometimes I'm like
a volcano –
all fiery, red and MEAN.
I run about and
YELL and SHOUT.
I get so MAD,
I SCREAM.

But....

Volcanoes spurt out

LAVA

and I'm NOT made of this.
And Mum can make me
calm right down
with cuddles
and a kiss.

I'm a bit like a computer.

There are LOTS of things I know —

like 3 + 5, my ABCs,

and what makes glow-worms GLOW.

But ...

Although we are *quite* similar,
there's just one minor hitch.
My dad points out that I don't have
a simple ON/OFF switch.

I'm like a lot of **different things**
and they're a LOT like me.
But I can't seem to pin it down:
Hmm, what makes me a ME?

No one else has got my **face**
or has my **hair** and **hands**...

Or thinks the **thoughts** inside my head
with all their SECRET plans.

No one dances
quite like Mum,

no one cooks
like Dad,

no one laughs
like Alfie Wilks,

Ha Ha HA HA!

and **all** this
makes me GLAD.

Everybody's DIFFERENT
in their own special way.
So, what makes me
a me is . . .

And that's the way I'll stay.